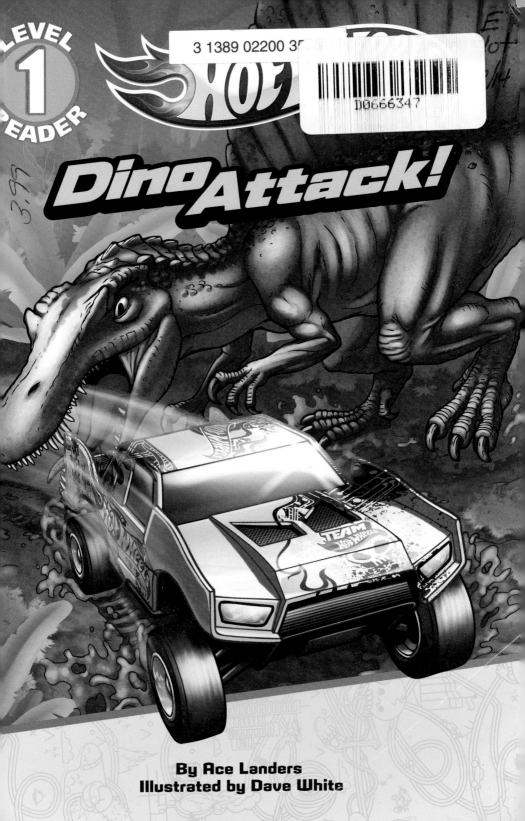

LEVEL 1 READER

Dino Attack!

By Ace Landers
Illustrated by Dave White

SCHOLASTIC INC.

ISBN 978-0-545-62542-5

HOT WHEELS and associated trademarks and trade dress are owned by, and used under
license from Mattel. Inc. © 2014 Mattel, Inc. All Rights Reserved.

Published by Scholastic Inc. SCHOLASTIC and associated logos
are trademarks and/or registered trademarks of Scholastic Inc.

12 11 10 9 8 7 6 5 4 3 2 1   14 15 16 17 18 19/0

Printed in the U.S.A.   08
First printing, January 2014

Team Hot Wheels
is going to an island.

The island has a secret track.

The blue driver scans the course.

The green driver revs his engine.

The red and yellow drivers are ready for anything.

But no one will win unless the gate opens.

Finally, it opens and the race begins!

The blue driver takes the lead.

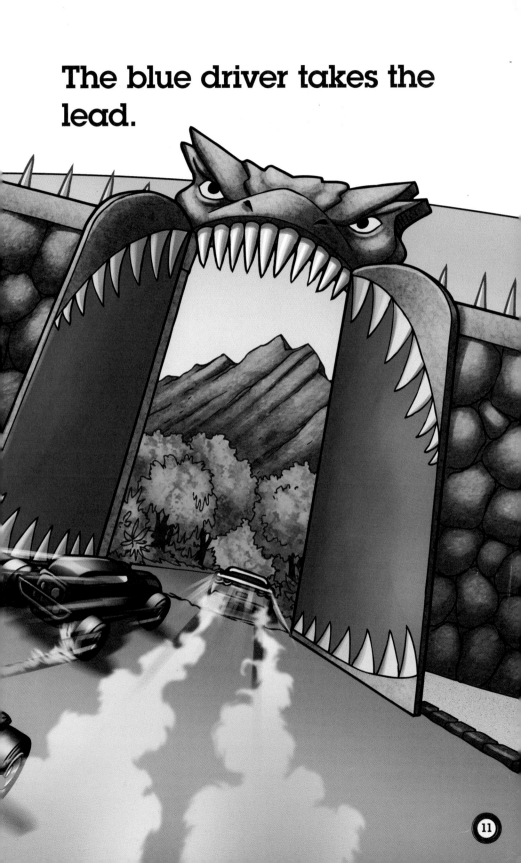

But the track is not finished!

The blue driver acts fast. A crane is in the perfect place!

The yellow and red drivers have a different idea.

The green driver puts the pedal to the metal. He makes the jump!

The drivers thought they were alone. But that is not true!

The yellow driver
dodges the dinosaur!

The green driver blasts
past the angry beast.

The dinosaur does not give up.

The helicopter comes to fly the racers home.

But the dino is on the attack!

The drivers must find
another way.

The blue driver heads for the dinosaur.

The red driver launches into the forest.

So does the yellow
driver.

The green driver shifts into overdrive.

The racers are running out of track!

But look . . . a ramp!

The drivers speed toward the ramp. It is their only escape.

They fly into the air and
land on the other side.

Team Hot Wheels survived the dino attack!